THE
GODDAUGHTER'S
REVENGE

THE GODDAUGHTER'S REVENGE

MELODIE CAMPBELL

RAVEN BOOKS
an imprint of
ORCA BOOK PUBLISHERS

Library and Archives Canada Cataloguing in Publication

Campbell, Melodie, 1955-
The goddaughter's revenge / Melodie Campbell.
(Rapid reads)

Issued also in electronic formats.
ISBN 978-1-4598-0487-6

I. Title. II. Series: Rapid reads
PS8605.A54745G632 2013   C813'.6   C2013-901925-1

First published in the United States, 2013
Library of Congress Control Number: 2013904965

Summary: When Gina discovers that someone has been switching
real gems with fakes in the jewelry of her best customers,
she takes matters into her own hands. (RL 3.8)

*Orca Book Publishers is dedicated to preserving the environment and has
printed this book on Forest Stewardship Council® certified paper.*

Orca Book Publishers gratefully acknowledges the support for
its publishing programs provided by the following agencies:
the Government of Canada through the Canada Book Fund and the
Canada Council for the Arts, and the Province of British Columbia
through the BC Arts Council and the Book Publishing Tax Credit.

Design by Teresa Bubela
Cover photography by Getty Images

ORCA BOOK PUBLISHERS
PO Box 5626, Stn. B
Victoria, BC Canada
V8R 6S4

ORCA BOOK PUBLISHERS
PO Box 468
Custer, WA USA
98240-0468

www.orcabook.com
Printed and bound in Canada.

16 15 14 13 • 4 3 2 1

For Dave, who has gamely put up with my whacky Italian family for decades.

CHAPTER ONE

Okay, I admit it. I would rather be the proud possessor of a rare gemstone than a lakefront condo with parking. Yes, I know this makes me weird. Young women today are supposed to crave the security of owning their own home.

But I say, Real estate, shmeel estate. You can't hold an address in your hand. It doesn't flash and sparkle with the intensity of a thousand night stars. It will never lure you away from the straight and narrow like a siren from some Greek odyssey.

Let's face it. Nobody has ever gone to jail for smuggling a one-bedroom-plus-den out of the country.

However, make that a ten-carat cyan-blue topaz with a past as long as your arm, and I'd do almost anything to possess it.

But don't tell the police.

* * *

Pete was sitting in my back office at Ricci Jewelers, poring over a tray of diamonds. Really nice diamonds. You could buy a whole condo building with those rocks.

"I like the big pear-shaped one. How much does that cost?"

"Too much," I said. "I'd be afraid to wear it. Might get mugged, you know?"

Pete looked over at me and raised one eyebrow. "By your own family?"

I grimaced. He had me on that one. Who was likely to mug the goddaughter of the local crime boss?

2

I sighed. "It's still too much." I swished a stray lock of hair behind my shoulder.

Pete pushed back from the table. He leaned back in the chair. His big hands went behind his head and linked there. I felt the familiar zing as his hazel eyes met mine.

"You know, this is rather like taking coals to Newcastle. You can buy any ring you want in your own store. Maybe I should buy you a car as an engagement gift."

I smiled at the quaint expression, then shook my head. "No sir, you're not getting out of this. Aunt Miriam always says you're not engaged until you've got the ring. So choose something, buster."

He smiled back and his eyes twinkled. "You choose something, gorgeous. We should do this together. Your budget is thirty thousand."

My jaw dropped. "Holy cannoli, Pete— how much do newspaper reporters make?"

A faint knock at the door made us both turn. It was Tiffany, my shop assistant. Her goth getup was somewhat alarming to many customers. Her face right now was even more alarming, and I don't mean from the piercings.

I signaled to her. She used her key to unlock the door.

"Sorry to interrupt," she said, "but you really need to see this."

She motioned toward the retail end of the store.

I stood up, grabbed my keys and walked around the desk. "Come see me in action," I said with a smile.

"I'd like to, but I really have to get back. Got a deadline." Pete sprang easily from the chair to his full six-foot-two height. I love to watch him move. He used to be a quarterback and has that perfect combination of strength and grace. Unusual in a big guy.

Pete turned around at the door. "You like the pear shape, right?"

"Oh yeah," I said. Who doesn't?

"How much is the big pear-shaped one?"

I met his eyes. They were smiling, just like his mouth.

"Twenty-four thousand," I said.

"Sold," he said. Then he grabbed me before I could pass through the door.

* * *

A minute or so later, Pete put me down. I was breathless. He waited for me to pass through the doorway and then shut the door behind us. It locked automatically. Then he continued out the store to the street beyond. I had to stop myself from running to the window to watch as he sauntered out of sight.

Instead, I drew my eyes back to the waiting customer.

An ultra-slim woman with shellacked red hair stood at the counter.

"Good morning, Mrs. Harris. How can I help you?" I said.

She smiled nervously. "The stone in my ring is a little loose. Can you fix it?"

"Of course," I said. A perfectly normal request and nothing to cause Tiff concern. I waited.

She held the ring out to me. I knew it, of course. A beautiful oval sapphire, surrounded by diamonds. Very Princess Di-ish. I'd sold it to her husband two years ago as an anniversary gift.

I held the ring between two fingers.

Mrs. Harris continued. "I had it in two weeks ago to get it appraised and cleaned. That nice cousin of yours from New York— the one who was here while you were away—did it for free. But then I noticed it was moving a bit. The stone, I mean."

I stared at the center stone. My mouth went dry. I reached for my loupe on the glass countertop.

I heard my voice, strained but controlled, say, "I can fix this, Mrs. Harris. Leave it with me. I'll phone you when it's ready."

Minutes passed. I didn't hear her leave the store. But when I looked up, Tiff was staring at me funny.

"Well?" said Tiff.

"You were right. It's a goddamn fake."

CHAPTER TWO

We stared at each other across the counter.

"Do you think she knows?" Tiff said. She twirled a strand of jet-black hair around her fingers.

I looked down at the ring.

"Not a chance. She wouldn't have brought it in if she did."

"I was thinking maybe she needed money or something. That she had a fake made so she could sell the real thing without her husband knowing."

I put down the loupe.

"More likely the husband did it. Maybe he needed money fast. Figured his wife wouldn't notice." And had no idea she would bring the ring to me, who *would* notice.

"What should we do?"

I looked off in the distance. Crap. No way could this turn out well.

"Not sure. Let me sleep on it."

* * *

Well, I tried to sleep that night. I tossed and turned, counted sheep and baby lambs. I dozed for a bit and then woke up with a start. The fake stone niggled at me. When had the switch taken place? And how the hell was I going to tell a client that her $20,000 sapphire ring was actually worth only the cost of the setting?

Sometime before dawn, the phone rang. I counted eight rings, then grabbed for it.

"Who died?" I yelled into the mouthpiece.

This was my standard response to night calls. On more than one occasion, it had been the right thing to say. Call it an occupational hazard.

The caller was Sammy the Stringbean. I could tell by the heavy breathing. Not *that* kind of heavy breathing. More like an asthmatic donkey with a head cold.

"Ha," he said. "Very funny. We got a problem." He seemed to think I'd care.

I groaned. "Not again. Not doing this. *You* got a problem. *We* don't got anything. *We* are going back to bed."

I had enough problems of my own, thank you. I didn't need to get mixed up in any more mob business. The last time had been a royal pain in the butt. Actually, make that *foot*.

No more sneaking hot gems across the border in my shoes! No sir. I wasn't even going to smuggle a donut into the States, if they asked me. Which they might, because our donuts are way better up here.

I heard a deep sigh.

Sammy is not a bad guy. I love him to pieces, in a niece-uncle way. He's far up the food chain in The Hammer, aka Steeltown, aka the industrial city of Hamilton. And he's my uncle Vince's cousin, which also makes him a second-cousin-in-law to me, or something. He's also Jewish, which means we can buy both our pastrami and our prosciutto wholesale in this family.

Usually, I am happy to give him the time of day. But this wasn't day. This was friggin' middle of the night, and I was a girl who valued her beauty sleep.

"So you got a problem," I mumbled. "I got a hundred of them, and they're all family."

This was true. I've got a lot of family, and they are "well-known" in The Hammer. And I am well-known for hating that fact.

11

Sammy cleared his throat. "Sugar, not this time. This time, the problem is yours. Meet you at the chicken coop in one hour. Bring your loupe."

* * *

Dawn was just breaking as I drove up the gravel path to the chicken coop. Of course, it isn't really a chicken coop. It's a two-bedroom cottage on the lakeshore in Stoney Creek. We call it the chicken coop because that's how it was registered for tax purposes. Chickens don't pay much tax. My cousin Maria works in the city tax-assessment department.

Sammy was already there. I passed by his shiny black Mercedes as I rounded the path to the front door. Sunlight sparkled off the lake before me. Gulls danced in the sky. I paused to listen to the lapping waves and then turned to enter the cottage.

I let the screen door slam behind me. Sammy was holding two coffee cups. He handed me one with double cream, no sugar.

"Thought we better meet here," he said. "Nobody to overhear. You won't want even the family to know about this."

I pulled the plastic lid off the coffee cup and took a swig. Good brew...hot and strong. Just the way I like my men. Which is not exactly how I would describe Sammy.

A single center light fixture was turned on, and the shades were drawn on all the windows. I stared at Sammy through the gloom and was reminded of Woody Allen. There was a lot going on behind those beady eyes.

I nodded to the left. "What's with the wall of cigarette cartons?"

They were stacked about six feet high and three feet deep against the side wall of the room.

"Had some trouble with a truck," Sammy said. He shifted his feet and slurped from the cup.

"Trouble being…the truck wasn't ours?"

Sammy shrugged. "They'll be gone by next week."

I let it go at that. My uncle Vince has a lot of businesses. Sammy is his right-hand man. I've found it's best to know as little as possible about businesses in the family. Except my own, of course.

I'm a certified gemologist and run a sweet little jewelry store that's been in the family for decades. It's all legit. I work hard to keep it that way. With my family, that's a feat.

I looked back at Sammy and waited. He reached into his pocket and pulled something out.

"Take a good look at this." He held it between two fingers and handed it to me.

I put my coffee down on a stack of cartons and took it from him. It was a rose tourmaline ring, about four karats, heart-shaped and surrounded by diamonds. Aunt Miriam's ring, which Sammy had purchased for her from my shop a few years ago. I pulled it closer and reached for the loupe in my pocket. I took a look.

"Shit!" I yelled. "What the fuck?"

"Hey, watch the language. Miriam don't like it when you talk like that."

"But—" I felt like hitting something. "It's a fake. Another one. Not even a good one. I did *not* sell you a fake. How the hell did this happen?"

But even as I said it, I knew the answer.

"Carmine." I felt like I'd been socked in the face. "That dweeb Carmine! He was minding the store for me a few weeks back, and he switched the stone. SONOVABITCH!" I was going to kill the bastard.

Carmine was a cousin from the New York branch of the family. He was a certified gemologist like I was, and Vince had brought him in to run the store while I was away.

Carmine would not have been my choice, in that he was about as weasely as a basket of weasels. We did not get on well as kids. Suffice it to say I used to call him Ratface and he called me Fat Bum.

So he wouldn't have been my choice, but Vince wanted to mend a few fences by accepting the offer of help that Big Sally had made. Recently there had been friction between certain factions of the extended family. I tried not to follow it too closely.

"You said *another one*. You mean there're more?" Sammy may look insignificant, but he's sharp as a hornet's stinger.

I placed the ring carefully into the little padded velvet bag I keep in my purse.

"One at least. I need to check."

Sammy swore. Good thing Aunt Miriam wasn't there to hear him.

"The little bastard has no brains at all. Stealing from us? He's gotta have a screw loose."

"He hates me. But even I didn't think he could be this low." Or stupid.

"You want I should tell Vinnie about this?" he said.

"No! No telling Vince. I can handle Carmine myself." Okay, that was a lie. What was I going to do? Tell his mother on him?

"We can't take him out, Sugar. He's Big Sally's son-in-law. It would start a war."

"No taking anyone out!" I hit my hand to my forehead. "That's the last thing I want. Especially after the recent trouble between Big Sally and Vince. No, let's keep this between just a few of us."

Not to mention that, if word got out, I would look like a complete loser to the rest of the family. Duped by that weasel Carmine. Yeah, maybe this was a stupid thing to worry about under the circumstances.

But it mattered to me. I had a rep to maintain inside the family *and* out.

"But maybe..." A bright glint came into Sammy's eyes. Now I was reminded of a leprechaun. "Let me see what we can dig up on him. Something you can use on him. Persuasion, if you get my drift. So you can get the real stones back."

I calmed down immediately. Blackmail. I liked it. It was crafty. "You got someone in New York who could maybe do a little research?"

Sammy smiled. "I got a hundred people in New York."

CHAPTER THREE

On my way to the store I called Pete. "Do you own a gun?" I said.

"Of course," he said smoothly. "I'm from Buffalo."

"Good. Because I may have to shoot someone."

* * *

A short time later, I was sitting in the office at Ricci Jewelers, considering ways to torture people. One person in particular. My cousin Carmine the Weasel.

Tiffany was focused on murder options. Tiff, my super-efficient, wardrobe-challenged, eighteen-year-old shop assistant also happens to be my uncle Manny's daughter. She dropped out of school this year because it was "pathetic." I am employing her because apparently I am a "good influence." Which only goes to show how "pathetic" things are in my family.

"We could boil him in oil."

"Too cliché," I said. I was checking our stock of precious stones for fakes. "Hand me that other tray."

"We could shove a cactus up his butt and make him sit on it." Her black-rimmed eyes sparkled at the thought.

Jesus, the young are bloodthirsty. At the moment, Tiff looks like a younger version of Winona Rider in *Beetlejuice*. By tomorrow she could be blond and dressed like Madonna. With Tiff, you never can tell.

I am told I look like Elizabeth Taylor playing Cleopatra on a really bad day— minus the blue eye shadow. For some reason, people think we look like sisters. I really don't know how to take that.

"I can't find any fakes here. What the hell was Carm up to?" I was baffled. The dweeb was behind this—I was sure of it.

Tiff shrugged. Her many piercings shrugged with her.

"Probably he just substituted a few fake stones in rings that he knew were leaving the store. He wouldn't have left anything fake here because he knows you would catch them when you came back."

A chill ran down my back. I put down the loupe.

"That's a brilliant deduction, Watson. I have an idea. Get me a list of items that were in for service during the time The Weasel was in charge of the store."

My head was spinning. I leaned forward in my chair, put both elbows on the desk and held my head in my hands.

"I never should have left the store," I mumbled to myself. "Never should have let Vince talk me into bringing the dweeb in to cover for me."

The thing is, I had to meet Pete's parents. We were engaged, for crissake. And you can't go to Florida from Hamilton for just a day—at least, not the first time, when they want to get to know you. Not to mention figure out what kind of nutcase their son has hooked up with. It wouldn't have been fair.

Pete's parents were delightful and obviously thrilled that Pete is settling down. His mother was a real sweetheart to me. Luckily, they have yet to figure out that I am a nutcase. Or that I come from a certain family.

Tiff returned with the list. We both pored over it.

Then I groaned and looked up.

"You know what this means?" I said.

Tiffany nodded. "Half The Hammer might be walking around with fake gems on their fingers."

I gulped. "And we have to get them back here and check each one before anyone finds out, or my rep is cooked."

"How are we going to do that?"

I stared into space. "Let me think."

CHAPTER FOUR

That evening, I assembled the vigilantes.

"We need a plan," I said to the group.

Tiff nodded. "A cunning plan."

I rolled my eyes.

The "group" was me, Tiff and her brother Nico, who was not gay but just liked the color pink. We were in Nico's teeny condo on Caroline Street. It was a short walk to Hess Village, the swank bar and bistro center of Hamilton. And yes, the condo was black and white with pink accents.

"Why isn't Sammy here?" said Nico. He was leaning against the black-granite countertop, nursing an espresso.

"I thought we'd just keep this between the three of us for now," I said cautiously. "Sammy has enough problems." And if Sammy became a part of this, then his wife—Aunt Miriam—would know about what we were doing, and Miriam would tell Aunt Vera, and then Vince—well, you get the picture.

Besides, Sammy was working another angle. I wanted him to concentrate on that.

First I had to solve the immediate problem. Which was to get the freaking fakes back from my clients. Then I could plan revenge.

"So we're all agreed," I said. "We have to get all the fake stones back and replace them with real ones before anyone finds out."

"Otherwise your reputation is toast," said Tiff.

I looked at her sideways.

"OUR reputation is toast. We lose our clientele, and you lose your job, sweetface."

I didn't want to think about that. I had worked hard to keep this business clean. So hard! And one rumor of fake stones would kill my rep for good. Crap, I was pissed!

I love my little store. It is just so *me*. Most jewelry stores are dark, rather dreary places with a lot of oak paneling. They look like old banks. Either that or they go the other way, with sleek black cabinets and annoying fluorescent lights. My store is bright-white and blue. Beautiful cyan-blue walls with sapphire accents. Glass shelves feature Murano glass sculptures shipped direct from Venice. Nico helped me with the makeover a year ago. One customer told me it's like walking into a gemstone. Gorgeous.

I didn't want to lose my store.

"How many invoices did you count again, Tiff?"

"Eight. Here's that list of items that came in during that week." She handed me the piece of paper we'd looked at before.

Aunt Miriam—check. Mrs. Harris—check. Then six more clients I knew well enough. They were regulars—and, unfortunately, some of Steeltown's elite. Definitely friends of my aunt Pinky.

"What did they bring them in for?"

"Cleaning and appraisal. Remember we ran that special for good clients last month?" Tiff said.

"Rats," I said. "So we can't entice them in here by offering the same deal. Too soon. Double rats."

I had two rings. That meant I had to get the other six and exchange the fake gems for real ones.

Sigh. This was going to cost me a fortune.

"Are you telling Pete?" Nico asked.

"Pete is that last one I'm going to tell!" I was firm about that. "He already thinks we're all wacko." Not to mention rather lacking in specific morals.

"Better we keep mum." I drummed my fingers on the desk. "After all, what I'm proposing is not exactly on the straight and narrow."

Silence. We'd all been thinking it. They'd been waiting for me to put it on the table and say out it out loud.

"So," I said slowly, "you're both with me?"

Nico nodded. He swished one hand airily through space. "Piece of cake. All those B and Es when I was a kid—I never got caught."

I held back a shiver. "Tiff?"

"I'm good. Whatever you need." Her dark brown eyes were glowing.

"Good." I took a breath. "So we're going to break into these houses and steal back the fakes."

CHAPTER FIVE

One day I am going to write a book. It's going to be entitled *Burglary for Dummies* and will have all sorts of helpful tips. Things like "Make sure your accomplices know the rules."

Nico arrived at the first target residence wearing all black. Black Gap T-shirt, black tight-fitting jeans, which were extra long because Nico is lanky, black shoes. I don't know where he managed to get black shoes like that. Maybe at a dance studio?

Of course, his hair is bleached bright blond, so the effort might have been wasted.

"Here I am!" he announced, all eager like a kid at Christmas. "Parked around the corner. Brought my tools." His small satchel was, of course, black, as were his gloves.

I sighed. He was really getting into this project, just as I feared.

"Now the idea is we get in and out quickly," I said. "According to Aunt Pinky, these people will be back tomorrow. I'm just going to switch the ring and vamoose. Got it?" I looked him square in the eyes. When had he started wearing black eyeliner?

"Roger," he said, and we walked up the path to the front door. "This is great, Gina! Been so long since I've done this. I feel just like Johnny Depp."

Now I was really having second thoughts. Make that third thoughts.

"You know this isn't a real burglary, right? We're not stealing anything. I'm actually replacing a fake with a real one."

Niko stopped at the door. He placed the satchel on the flagstone step and pulled out something small and made of steel. "That's what makes it so much fun," he said, working the lock. "No need to find a fence, and I get to see how the rich decorate their houses."

"How is that interior-design course going, by the way?" I asked.

There was a *click* and a *ting*. Nico turned the weathered brass knob and the door swung open.

"Oh dear," he said as he walked in.

"What?" I was right behind him and immediately on the alert.

"Don't turn on a light. I don't think I can stand it." He waved a slim hand at the living room in front of us.

I followed the gesture. Nothing there but a whole lot of furniture. Not very nice furniture—rather heavy—and the room was far too crowded. But no dogs or feral cats around that I could see.

I gave a sigh of relief. "Okay, you keep watch. I'll be upstairs in the master bedroom. Buzz my cell if you need to alert me."

Nico sniffed. "This is a disaster. Look at those tacky coral pillows. That awful throw rug covering perfectly good hardwood. All this money, and the place looks like it was decorated out of an eighties catalog. I'm appalled, Gina. Absolutely appalled."

"You just stay right there!" I commanded, taking the stairs two at a time. "I won't be a minute."

I was more than a minute, of course. This was a big home, and the master bedroom was at the opposite end of the second floor. It took me about sixty steps to get to it. I looked in at least five bedrooms and two bathrooms along the way. There were two guest rooms, a computer room and a room totally done—make that overdone—in hot pink. You don't want to know what the boy's room was like. I hastily closed the door.

I opened the double doors that led to the master. It was about the size of a baseball field and just as nicely decorated as the living room. I didn't stop to admire the faded floral matching drapes and bedspread.

It took me a little time to find the ring. First I tried the jewelry boxes in plain sight. Nothing there but tacky costume jewelry. Of course, many people do that to fool burglars into thinking there's nothing of value in the place. But I knew different, so I dug deeper. The emerald ring was in the top middle drawer of the French provincial dresser, under a pile of lingerie. Calling it lingerie was generous. Mrs. Hewitt obviously kept her undies until they fell down.

The ring was in a Ricci Jewelers box, which made me feel good for some reason. I made the switch and pushed in the drawer. Then I listened.

Strange noises were coming from downstairs. Drat that Nico—he must have turned on the television.

I retraced my steps to the master bedroom doors and closed them gently behind me. The trick to a successful break and enter is to leave everything exactly as one found it.

Crreek!

I hurried to the stairs.

Clunk.

I ran down the stairs and stopped dead on the last one.

"Nico, what the hell?"

The brown sofa had been moved to the back of the room, against the expansive picture window. The carpet was gone, and at least two chairs were missing. The coffee table had been cleared of all but one art book. A turquoise pashmina was draped artfully across the cream loveseat.

"Isn't this better?" said Nico. "I moved the icky chairs to the dining room and removed those awful pillows. Couldn't do much about the paintings, of course. But now, with the sofa moved, the focus is on the great view out the back."

I gulped. "You rearranged their furniture?"

"It was either that or kill myself. I couldn't spend another moment in this place, Gina."

I hit my head with my hand. I was still searching for words when the telephone rang. Not my cell, but the telephone in the house.

"Let's get out of here," he whispered. We rushed out the front door, and Nico discreetly turned the lock with his little tool. At the sidewalk, we parted as planned and took separate cars home. This was probably a good thing, because for the first time in my life I was truly speechless.

* * *

Saturday morning, Pete got up first. I like it when he does that. Coffee is already made by the time I amble into the kitchen. I discovered early on that Pete is a full-service boyfriend.

As expected, Pete was reading the paper. Usually he starts with the sports section. But today, he was staring at the front page.

I walked over to get myself coffee. Pete made a strange sound, so I turned before reaching the counter.

Pete's face changed. First it was a frown. Then it split to a grin. Then his mouth twisted and he handed the paper to me.

"Your family got anything to do with this?"

The headline screamed: *The Lone Rearranger—Who Was That Masked Man?*

Under it was a photo of a white silk bandit mask, artfully arranged across the back of a brown sofa. I knew that sofa. I had seen it recently. It was the one in the Hewitt house.

"CRAP!" I yelled. I read more.

Hamilton residents were shocked to discover that someone had broken into their home Thursday night to rearrange the living room furniture.

"Nothing was taken," said Mr. Hewitt, "so we have to assume that he just hated the way the place looked. So did I. This guy has talent."

Mrs. Hewitt was delighted with the new arrangement. "It's so much more spacious-looking. I really like the editing he did. And that turquoise pashmina! I never thought of putting brown and cream and turquoise together, but it goes so well. Now I want to try some new colors."

Police are calling the suspect The Lone Rearranger because of the Lone Ranger-type mask the intruder left behind.

"Crappity CRAP!" I dropped the news-paper on the kitchen island. "I'm gonna kill him."

"Care to explain?"

My eyes moved to Pete. He had one eyebrow raised and a whole lot more going on with his face.

"Sonovabitch," I muttered and reached for the phone.

Nico answered on the first ring.

"Isn't it exciting?" he said. "Front page, even! I can't wait to tell Jordy."

"No! No telling anyone!" I was pacing now. Pacing and fuming. "That pashmina was yours? And you left it there?"

He clicked his tongue. "It just came to me. A hit of saturated color is so modern, and turquoise is the new gray. It goes with almost everything. I always carry a couple in my satchel. But don't worry. I wore gloves, remember?"

Pete was looking at me strangely. "Are you okay?" he mouthed.

Nico continued talking. "Wasn't the mask a nice touch? I wanted to surprise you. At first, I couldn't make up my mind between black or white, but then white seemed more original, you know?"

I was hyperventilating now. "Nico, you are NOT the Pink Panther! This was supposed to be a covert operation."

"Do you think maybe next time I could leave a bill behind?"

CHAPTER SIX

Saturday afternoon was good. Tiff was busy with a customer when I got to the store. I waved a hand at her and went directly to the back room.

This was going to be a great day. This was the day I was setting my own engagement ring. And it was a doozie. Never in my life had I expected to wear such a diamond. Can't explain it exactly, but it does something to a girl.

When Tiff was done with the customer, she joined me in the back room. I was poring over settings.

"I think this one." The band I picked up was narrow yellow gold with three prongs. One prong would cover the point end of the pear-shaped diamond, to protect it.

"Yeah," said Tiff. "Simple. Will really show it off."

"I like white gold," I said, hesitating. "But somehow yellow gold seems more wedding-like, if you know what I mean."

"Yellow gold blends in with flesh color," she said. "White gold stands out against it. So if you want the band to stand out, you pick white gold. If you want the stone to be prominent, use yellow."

I lifted my head and stared at her. "Well done, little cuz. I'm impressed. How did you pick that up so fast?"

She looked really pleased. "I've been watching. And experimenting. For instance, I can see just by looking that this is a beaut." She pointed to my diamond, sitting on the velvet mat. "What are the specs?"

"Vvs1. Color grade, D. Cut, excellent. Check it out yourself." I handed her the loupe.

After a few moments, she whistled low. "That's impressive. I really like this business."

"You should go for your certification," I suggested.

She nodded slowly. "I'm thinking about it."

The front-door bell jingled, announcing another customer. Tiff rose to greet her. I set about my main task, humming to myself all the while.

* * *

That night at dinner, Pete popped a question.

"What do you think about the Saturday before Christmas?"

We were sitting in La Paloma on James, my uncle Vito's restaurant. It was sort of our place. By that I mean Pete's and mine. Luckily, he loves Italian food. Luckily, my uncle Vito likes Pete. Vito likes his food, too, and has the belly to prove it.

La Paloma is "uptown cool" for Hamilton. Not your little Ma and Pa place. It has the best wine cellar in the city. Many high-priced business deals are signed here, and not just those in the family.

But Pete was asking about the Saturday before Christmas, so I decided to stop munching bruschetta for just a moment to answer.

I looked up and met his hazel eyes. "Prime shopping time, but I'm usually done by then. I like it fine. What are you talking about?"

"My parents come home for two weeks around Christmas. I thought it would be a nice time to get married."

My jaw dropped. "So soon?"

Both his eyebrows rose in alarm. "Don't you want to?"

I swallowed hard. "Of course I do. I meant, how are we going to get a hall that soon? They're booked a year in advance."

Pete relaxed. "Got that all worked out. I called Sammy and explained the situation. He knows the manager at the Forum. They've got a cancelation. I told him to reserve it on spec."

"Sure he knows the manager," I said. I wiped my mouth with the linen napkin. "We own the place. Didn't you know that?"

He just smiled.

I just hoped the people who had originally booked the place weren't "canceled."

Then another thought hit me.

"But," I wailed, "I don't have a wedding dress yet!"

Now he laughed. "It's still two months away. You can find something in that time."

"Are you kidding? Haven't you ever seen that TV show *Say Yes to the Dress*? It takes at least three months to order a dress. And for crissake, Pete, everyone will think I have to get married if we do it that soon!"

Yikes! Aunt Miriam thinking I *had* to get married. I shivered.

Pete sighed. He pushed back from the table. "I thought you'd be pleased."

He looked so disappointed—just like a little boy. I think it was the most surprised I'd ever been in my life.

I couldn't stand it. I relented immediately. I guess that's how you know you really love someone.

"Okay," I said. My voice was deliberately light and happy. "The Saturday before Christmas. Let's do it. You book the hall. I'll find a dress somehow."

A big smile split his face. "Great! Now will you please give me the ring so I can put it on your finger?"

I smiled back. I reached into my purse and pulled out a blue velvet Ricci Jewelers box. I snapped it open and passed it to him. Pete lifted the ring out of its case and whistled.

"Knock-out stone for my gorgeous gal. This is for keeps, babe." He reached across the table for my left hand.

Of course, that was the very minute Uncle Vito decided to pop out from the kitchen to bring the pasta verde in person.

"Vera!" He yelled across the crowded restaurant. "He's giving her the ring! Get out here!"

Vera came running from the kitchen, wiping her hands on a dishtowel. She was followed by several of the cooking staff.

"Stella! Call Miriam and Pinky, and Maria in Florida! She's got the ring!" Vera hollered to the hostess at the front, another cousin of mine.

And that's when the circus started.

* * *

We didn't get home until after midnight. Everyone in the resto came over to congratulate us. Vito got out the Prosecco—bottles of it.

Many toasts were made. The smart phones came out and photos were up on Facebook within minutes. Then our cell phones started ringing.

Pete got louder with every slap on the back, and I got tipsy. I inadvertently spilled the news about the date, and Vera started phoning the family to mobilize. Pinky would hold the shower. Stella would arrange the invitations. Vera would be in charge of food, of course. Luca would do the music. And Miriam would handle the guest list (God help anyone who was invited but didn't come).

My job was to find a dress.

Pete's job was to show up on the day. "If I don't show up, you'll know I'm dead," he assured me.

"If you don't show up, you *will* be dead," I said knowingly.

CHAPTER SEVEN

In my book *Burglary for Dummies*, there is going to be a chapter called "The Art of Blackmail." Personally, I don't hold with blackmail as a career choice. But there are times when mutual blackmail can be mutually beneficial.

It was Sunday afternoon. Pete was glued to the television, watching football. I waved a hand and told him I was going to the store. That was a lie.

I really didn't need Nico for this burglary, because I already had the front-door key. How? Well, you see my uncle Vince happens to own this housecleaning company called Maids-a-Go-Go. Yup, it is darn handy having a cleaning company in the family.

But it's always good to have a wingman in case things go wrong. So I called Nico and told him to meet me at this address in Aldershot.

I'd done my research. Mrs. Wilson had canceled their cleaning for Wednesday. That meant they weren't going to be around. People often do that to save money if they're going away. Why pay for a house to be cleaned if you aren't going to be there for a while?

And no security alarm. I knew that because the Maids were able to use the key to get in while Mrs. Wilson was out shopping and didn't have to worry about setting off alarms. She went shopping a lot.

To be honest, the Wilson house probably didn't merit an alarm. It was in a nice area of Aldershot, but it wasn't a showstopper.

Nico stood gazing at it, then gave a long sigh. "I'm not looking forward to this one, Gina. I mean, really. Look at that exterior."

Long, low brick bungalow in an unappealing baby-poop brown. Not a lot of money had been spent on the thing in, say, thirty years. The current Mrs. Wilson was the second Mrs. Wilson, and a lot younger than her husband. It was rumored that all his money got spent on her upkeep.

"Just don't move anything," I ordered.

"Probably isn't anything worth moving, except to the trash," Nico muttered.

I walked up to the front door, Nico following reluctantly. The key worked like a charm. I opened the door and stepped in.

No dogs to worry about. I'd checked that out too.

The living room was directly ahead, and the drapes were closed. "They're away in Vegas, according to Maids-a-Go-Go. Chances are she didn't take the ring.

Most people don't take their best stuff when they travel." I felt it my duty to educate Nico, since he was younger than me.

The kitchen was to the left. The bedrooms were down a dark hallway to my right. The master bedroom was at the end.

"You wait here while I search the master bedroom. DON'T MOVE ANYTHING!"

Nico stared mournfully at the living room. He moaned as if truly in pain.

"It's too awful. Look at that flower brocade from the eighties."

I was already moving down the hall. The door to the master was ajar. The blinds were closed, so I slipped through the doorway and fumbled for the light switch with my right hand.

Flick.

"What the hell?"

My eyes followed the voice. A figure turned over on the bed.

I stared.

"EEEK!" shrieked a female voice. "Eddie?"

Oops. It appeared not everyone who lived in this house was on vacation. One rather well-endowed male was vaulting off the bed. He didn't have any clothes on. And he wasn't Mr. Wilson. Worse, I knew him. Worse, so did Nico.

"Uncle Manny?" I squeaked.

"DAD?" Nico had raced up behind me.

The man in question froze like a statue. His head whipped around. He squinted.

"Gina? NICO? What the fuck are you doing here?"

"More to the point, what are YOU doing here?" Actually, it was pretty clear what he had been doing here, but I left out the operative word.

"Dad! Oh. My. God. I can't look." Nico brought up his right hand dramatically to cover his eyes.

"Ah, Nico. Ah, crap." Manny grabbed for the sheets to cover his boy bits. The woman on the bed grabbed them back. I watched the two of them pull back and forth. I thought about turning the lights off. There were far too many things wobbling.

"Manny, if you set me up for blackmail, I will parboil your pecker!" Mrs. Wilson was sitting up now. She had caramel hair, and her do was pretty messed up. Even angry, she was pretty, like Ginger from *Gilligan's Island*. I tried to ignore the swinging bazoombas.

"Babe, I didn't set up nothing. Gina, what the fuck is going on?"

My eyes swung back to my uncle, who is about fifty years old with a full head of curly salt-and-pepper hair. His handsome face was twitching.

Nico said, "I can't take this, Gina. I'm going to throw myself on that disgusting couch in the living room until you're done. Maybe I'll get the plague from it and die. That would be better than WHAT I SEE HERE!"

He marched out of the room, his head held high.

I felt sorry for Nico, I really did. But this was actually a piece of luck. True, I had no right to be in that room. But since the party in front of me had even less right to be there...

Time to improvise. The ring was in my pocket. I reached in with one hand.

I shrugged and smiled. "Just doing a bit of reverse burglary."

I turned to Ginger. "Mrs. Wilson, here's your emerald ring back. Somebody stole it. Switched it with a fake. They tried to sell the real one to me at the store, and I recognized it. I'm returning it."

Okay, so that was a big fat lie. I'm going to hell, just like the nuns said. But so are Uncle Manny and most of my family, so we should have a good time there.

I walked over to the bed and handed it to her.

"Here's the real one. You can keep the fake too."

Her manicured hand reached out and snatched it.

"Why, aren't you sweet! Look at that, Manny! I didn't even know it had been stolen. Talk about service."

Manny squinted at me. He didn't buy a word of it. Tough. I had one up on him.

"Aunt Grizelda know you're here?" I said sweetly.

His face went white. "Don't you dare."

He was right. I wouldn't dare. I was plum scared of Aunt Griz. If you think the men in our family are dangerous, wait till you meet the women.

But I still had the upper hand.

"This is simple, really." I walked back to the doorway. "I mean, we're family and all. Let's make a deal. I don't tell anyone you were here, and you don't tell anyone I was here."

"Done." Manny dropped the sheet and bent over to reach for his pants on the floor. I turned away but not quick enough. *Eeeyuuu.*

"And can I recommend that you don't come here ever again? For Nico's sake. I can probably keep him from spilling this time, but if you keep it up…"

"Done and done," said Manny. He sat down on the bed and stuck one leg in his pants. Then the other. He swept an arm across his forehead. He looked relieved— strangely relieved. I had to wonder if it was because I had promised not to tell or because he wouldn't have to come here again.

Mrs. Wilson had obviously missed this last exchange. She was still staring at her ring. "Wow, this is a nice emerald," she said. "I'd forgotten how big it was."

No kidding, it was nice. The original had been one carat. I didn't have anything in the store exactly that size, so I'd had to replace it with a bigger one. Yet another loss for the business. I was going to murder Carmine.

But first I had to get the rocks back.

CHAPTER EIGHT

In *Burglary for Dummies*, I'm going to have a chapter on chickens. Basically, on not counting them before they hatch. Otherwise known as overconfidence.

Nico had a college class on Tuesday, so I recruited Tiffany to be my wingman. Or wing-goth. She certainly dressed the part without trying. Black on black, with a side order of chains.

"The simplest ways are the best," I explained patiently to Tiff. We were parked in front of a long, low bungalow not far off Plains Road. "The best way to get in is to be invited."

"You're kidding," said Tiff. She didn't try to mask her disappointment. No Robin Hood tricks today.

"Not at all," I said smugly. "Piece of cake. It's always easier returning jewelry than stealing it in the first place." The fake stone had been replaced, and I was merely escorting it home, in a manner of speaking.

"How did you manage to lift the ring?"

I grinned. "Maids-a-Go-Go. I got Aunt Pinky to invite Mrs. Harmon over for coffee while they were cleaning her house. All of Pinky's friends use our cleaning service because we give them a deal. I nipped over here when she was out."

"Awesome."

I liked hearing that respect in her voice.

"Just watch me," I said, "and keep your cell phone on." I grabbed my black business case and swung open the car door.

"Then what do you do? Once you're in?" she asked.

"Ask to use the washroom. Pretend to leave, but instead find a place to hide. Then I just wait until she goes to another part of the house. I leave the ring somewhere in a place she might take it off. Like by the kitchen sink. Then I get out. I'll be quick."

I slammed the car door and headed up the drive.

"Hello, Mrs. Harmon," I said. The door had opened to a short fifty-something woman with petrified blond hair. "I'm from Ricci Jewelers. I believe you were there for a ring cleaning a few weeks ago? We forgot to give you this thank-you gift." I handed her a small brown box wrapped tightly with packing tape.

"Why, thank you, dear! This is a nice surprise." Her little pig eyes stared greedily at the box.

"Excuse me," I whispered, "but would you mind if I used the powder room before I go?"

"Not at all. It's right that way," she said, pointing. "I'll just run down to the kitchen for scissors to open this." And she scurried off down the hall.

I opened and closed the washroom door for the right sound effect, then looked for my favorite place to hide—don't ask me where; I plan to use it again.

I heard Mrs. Harmon padding back to the marble foyer.

"Thank you very much, dear—oh!" She realized she was talking to an empty room. I imagined her peering in the washroom. I waited. There was a moment's silence, then a few shuffles and the sound of jingling keys. Four electronic beeps and a clunk.

61

A door opened and closed. Then came the unmistakable sound of a garage-door opener, and a car firing up.

Crap! I thought. Crap, crap, double crap. I flipped open my cell.

"I have a slight problem," I whispered to Tiff. "She set the alarm and left by the garage door. It's one of those inside sensor things. I can see a little box over the bay window. I'm afraid to move. If I try to leave, the sensors will catch me, and the alarm will go off!"

A pause. "Can you see any sensors behind you?" Tiff said.

"Doesn't matter," I explained bitterly. "If I try to open any door or window, it will trip. That's how these things work."

Another pause.

"She wasn't supposed to leave," I wailed.

"Don't panic," she said finally. "I know just who to call. Back in a sec." *Click.*

"Don't call! Tiff—don't call anyone! Do you hear me? Tiff? Crap."

I stood with my cell phone on Standby and tried not to breathe.

It's a funny thing about time. Minutes slow right down when you can't move. Seconds take twice as long as they should. They just meander about, enjoying the scenery and lazing along as if nothing matters at all.

Try standing still for several minutes without moving. It's not easy. Everything itches. Molecules you didn't even know you had itch. My head itched. The instep of my left foot itched. I tried to distract myself by naming all the itchy parts of my body in French. No doubt about it—ten years of public-school core language down the drain. Then the phone rang.

"Where are you?" I yelled into it.

"At the office. Am I supposed to be somewhere?" It was Pete, and he sounded puzzled. Crap!

"Oh hi!" I recovered quickly and far too cheerfully. "Sorry—I was expecting Nico to phone." Just add that lie to my collection of sins. "Can I call you back? I'm sort of stuck at the moment." At least that part was true.

He hung up, and I stopped hyperventilating.

A short while later, the front door swung open and Tiff walked in.

"Yo there," she said cheerfully. "A-team to the rescue. Everything's cool. My friend Stoner fixed the alarm."

"Who's Stoner?" I said.

This became apparent the moment I said it. In trailed a tall thin guy with long stringy hair and glazed eyes. In came also the unmistakable aroma of freshly smoked something. Oh, and a dog. A very big black dog.

"Is that a black standard poodle with a mohawk?" I said, staring.

"Yeah, man," Stoner drawled. He grinned slowly. "Toker's such a cool dude dog, real smart, ya know, and he needed an image that kinda reflects, ya know…uh…him."

I reached down to scratch the black beast—not far, because his head came up to my waist—and he waggled appreciatively. His mohawk felt like velvet, and it balanced the long floppy ears in a zany way. I love all dogs, but big soft shaggy ones are impossible to resist.

"Suits him," I said with a chuckle. "Can't imagine why more poodle owners don't go in for punk." Good grief. What would they say at the Westminster? "What did you call him?"

"Toke," Stoner said slowly, drawing out the vowel. He seemed to do everything in slow motion. "Toker, for short."

That figures, I thought to myself.

"Tiff, you weren't supposed to tell anyone." I started out the back door and signaled for them to follow.

"Had to," said Tiff. "But don't worry about Stoner. He's cool. Nico and Stoner used to hang out in high school. He knows everything about alarm systems."

"I won't tell anyone," Stoner said dreamily. "But I can't speak for Toker."

"Woof!" barked the dog happily.

We made an amusing entourage, creeping down the sidewalk and out to the road like a pack of high-school kids taking a shortcut through the houses en route to school.

I stopped dead in panic. There was a white panel van marked *Stonehouse Security* parked right across the road. Damn! And the kids were with me. Could this day get any worse?

Tiff walked to the van and opened the back door for Toke to jump in. "Stoner's Dad owns a security company. That's how he knows about alarm systems and everything."

"Yeah," said Stoner happily. "Pretty neat, huh?"

"Pretty neat," I echoed.

Unbelievable, I thought to myself. I want what he smokes.

* * *

That night, the phone rang a lot.

First it was Pete. "Got a game tonight and tomorrow. I'll stay at my apartment. Can you live without me?"

God, his voice did something nice to my insides.

"Sure," I said, trying to sound sultry. "I'll just call up my B list."

"Do that and I'll have to commit murder," he said.

I laughed nervously. That word again. It kept creeping up.

Next, Sammy called.

"I made some rather interesting connections in New York," he said. "Re our mutual rat friend. Looks like I could have something for you soon."

"Great," I said. "I'll be ready."

CHAPTER NINE

Fourth time lucky, right? Wrong.

Another tip in the future bestseller *Burglary for Dummies* will be "Always case the place to make sure it's empty before you break in."

It was a good thing Pete had a game to watch the next evening, because I had a job to do.

I picked Nico up at seven. The sun was just setting. Nice thing about October— the sun sets earlier. It's easier for cat burglars to get around in the dark without being noticed.

"No security system on this place, so we don't need Stoner," Nico said. "Traveling light today." He patted the black leather pouch at his waist.

"Promise me something," I said. "No moving furniture this time either, okay?"

Nico sighed. "You're no fun at all."

This house was in the tony area of Red Hill. I parked around the corner from the property. There were two other cars parked in front of me.

"This is good. We're well out of sight." I gestured to Nico to show him the way.

We walked nonchalantly down the sidewalk, just two young people out for a walk. At the target property, we turned and strode up the path to the front door.

Nico took a set of keys from his pouch. He eyed the lock and then selected a key. In it went. He turned it and pushed the door. It swung open.

"First key I used—how crazy is that? Never happens. Must be our lucky day." He was all cheery.

That didn't last long.

Nico walked in first. I was right behind him and pulled the door closed. I could hear voices coming from the living room. The television was on or something. Some people do that to make you think they're at home.

Nico gasped and put a hand to his throat.

"Uh—Gina? We're not alone."

Two goons were looking right at us. They looked mean. There was a third guy, as big as a dump truck and probably just as classy. Worse, I knew him.

"Gina?"

Crap. Joey Battalia, my Buffalo cousin. And—wait for it—Bertoni, the creepy, slimy guy I'd most like to nominate for Whack the Wanker. The one who had made my life miserable in what Pete likes to call *The Great Shoe Fiasco.* I preferred to think of that episode as "Gina bails out the family, as usual."

Bertoni still had the greasy hair. And the charm of a wood louse.

"Christ, Lou, it's the crazy broad with the shoes," Bertoni said to the other goon.

I didn't even bother to acknowledge them.

"Joey, for crissake, you're supposed to be in Buffalo. What the hell are you doing here?" I yelled, flinging my arms around.

Joey snorted. "What the fuck does it look like?" He put his big fists on his hips. "You got a monopoly on The Hammer?"

I stared at Joey. Then I closed my eyes to wish him away. Didn't happen. He was still in front of me, all three hundred pounds of him, when I opened them.

"This isn't fair," I said, waggling a finger in his face. "You're freaking American. Go work in your own country, why don't you?"

And then I had another thought. "Does my uncle know you're doing this?"

"Of course he does. I'm not stupid."

Uh-oh. This made things rather awkward. I looked away. The problem was, Joey wasn't stupid at all. The other problem was, Uncle Vince didn't know I was doing this. And it would take Joey mere moments to put two and two together...

"Holy shit! That means Vince doesn't know YOU'RE doing this! HA!" He started to laugh. "Hey Bertoni! We got somethin' on her."

Bertoni grinned—at least, I think it was a grin—but it was pretty clear he didn't get it. He looked pained. His skeletal face obviously wasn't meant for smiling.

"I'm NOT doing this. STOP that. I don't break into houses and steal things. I'm just replacing a fake ring with a real." It was simple. I had to stop that stupid laughter. I also had to do the switch and get out of there before I accidently killed someone.

"You mean you're stealing a real ring and replacing it with a fake." He shook his head.

"Nope. I meant it the first time."

"Huh? I don't get it."

"Do you think we could sit down to discuss this?" Nico said. He put a hand to his head. "I've had a fright, and I'm feeling a little weak from lack of coffee."

I rolled my eyes. "Can we get going here? I just need to make this switch and then we can leave you alone to do whatever you want to do." Believe me, I wanted to get out of there. I never wanted to see those losers again.

"Where's the boyfriend?" Joey asked.

I didn't answer.

"I heard you were hot and heavy. So why isn't he here instead of Fancy Pants?"

"Hey! I'm right here, remember? Oh. I guess that doesn't have to be an insult." Nico looked confused.

I pretended to be deaf.

So Joey laughed again. A big hoarse chortle. "He doesn't know you're doing this either. Shit, this is a hoot."

"Shut up!" I hissed like a harpy. "Shut your fat face!"

Bertoni started to laugh then. He sounded like a hyena. Then the third guy joined in.

I hate being laughed at. This is when I went a little crazy. I picked up a china figurine that had been sitting on the oak end table and whacked Joey over the head with it.

"Fuck!" he yelled. "What are you doing?" One huge hand went to his scalp to massage the injured spot.

The china skirt was now in several pieces on the floor. I was left with a head in my hand.

"Hold it right there, Gina." Nico grabbed my arm before I could pick up anything else. "That was a Doulton you just wrecked."

I shook him off. Then I turned and stalked off, my head held high.

"Bloody cousins," I muttered as I stomped down the hall to the bedroom wing. All I wanted to do was switch a little ring to make things right. And now they would probably steal the damn thing, after all my trouble—

Wait a minute. If Joey and gang were going to steal it, why didn't I just keep it? Then I'd recover some of the money I'd lost because of that dweeb Carmine.

I entered the master bedroom and went straight to the jewelry box on the dresser. There it was—the fake ring. I took it just in case. No sense leaving a trail of fakes. But I didn't leave the real ring in its place.

This joint was in the process of being burgled. The cops would assume the ring had been taken by the real thieves.

I walked back to the living room feeling pretty smug.

Joey, Bertoni, Lou and Nico were crowded around a glass display cabinet.

It was kind of weird. Nico appeared to be giving a lesson in valuables.

"This china figurine stuff—it's pretty commonplace." Nico sniffed. "Ignore that stuff. Now this…" He pointed to a crystal statue. "This is Lalique. Gorgeous. And super valuable. Be real careful with it." He picked it up reverently.

Bertoni looked amazed. "How do you know all this shit?"

"*Antiques Roadshow*, of course. Every day I would rush home from school and watch it on the telly. Didn't you guys?"

Joey shook his head.

"Really." Nico tch-tched. "*Antiques Roadshow* should be required viewing for all aspiring break-and-enter artists. You have to do your homework, guys. Otherwise you end up stealing crap."

Joey said something, and then we heard a strange metallic squeaking sound.

We all stopped moving. Nobody said a word. The squealing continued.

EEEEEEEYIEEEE

"It's the garage-door opener," Nico cried. "Everybody run!"

Bertoni and Lou went wide-eyed, like crazy men. They dropped the china dolls they had been holding. Both Doultons hit the hardwood floor and shattered.

Joey turned quickly and smashed into a spindly side table. It went crashing over, dumping more figurines on the floor.

Bertoni leaped over the fallen table and hit the back of the couch, shifting its position. Joey was right behind him, with Lou on his tail. Lou tripped on something and a lamp went flying.

They had the patio doors open by the time I got my legs moving. Nico sprinted through the wreckage and beat me to the doors. I noticed he still had the Lalique in his hand. We all raced for the ravine behind the house. We spilled into the Red Hill Valley and scattered through the brush, just like we'd all been taught to do.

* * *

It was completely black outside when I finally stopped running. No stars and hardly any moon. I was breathing so hard, my heart was slamming against my chest wall.

No one else was in sight. I pulled out of the green nature stuff onto a path and surveyed the damage. My neck itched. Something had bitten it and was coming back for more. There were odd bits of foliage in my hair. I moved farther out of the bush and made for a streetlight. This road didn't seem familiar. These bunga-lows were much smaller than the ones on Country Club Drive, and older than Elvis. I walked the length of the block, until I hit a Stop sign. My brain recorded the road names, but they didn't ring a bell. I had no idea how far I was from my car or which direction to walk in order to get back to it.

Luckily, I had my cell phone in my pocket. I thought about calling a cab. But I didn't want there to be a taxi record of me going back to the vicinity of the break-in. So I called another number.

Tiff wasn't answering. I thought about it for a few seconds. No one else knew I was doing this, not even Sammy. I really didn't want to bring the family into this.

So I called another number.

"I need a ride," I said. I gave the names of the crossroads and then sat down on the curb to wait.

Pete pulled up in his convertible about ten minutes later. The top was down. He waited until I had plunked myself into the seat and fastened the seat belt. He stared at me. He tried to look stern. Maybe it was the fact that my hair was a rat's nest.

Maybe it was that I couldn't stop scratching my neck and swearing. His face twisted into a grin, then went back to being serious.

"I just spent an hour trying to get out of the stupid valley," I said.

"Never mind," he said, picking something out of my hair. "You brought back some of it with you."

He threw whatever it was over the side of the car. I didn't ask if it was animal, vegetable or mineral.

"Where's the Lone Rearranger?" he said finally.

"He took another route." I said, closing the door.

*　*　*

Later the next day, Nico told me that the noise in question wasn't a garage-door opener after all. It was the furnace coming on. He had deliberately fooled us because he was getting concerned that the double burglary was going to end badly. By this he meant all of us being hauled down to the cop shop. This had worried him because he had a class in color theory the next day. He was really looking forward to that class.

Of course, the incident made the Friday paper.

Lone Rearranger Targets Living Room

Hamilton residents are stunned to learn that the Lone Rearranger has struck again, breaking in last night to a home in Red Hill and trashing the living room.

Very little was taken, but furniture was overturned and several figurines were smashed.

"I'm mortified," said Mrs. O'Brien, owner of the home where the break-in occurred. "This is such an embarrassment, being targeted in this way. I thought the room was charming. I guess he didn't like it. Nobody told me shabby chic was out. What will my friends think?"

"I hated all those knickknacks. Now maybe she'll listen to me," said Mr. O'Brien.

Police believe the intruder…

"Don't you think it's about time you told me exactly what's going on?" Pete said smoothly.

I gulped, then started to spill.

CHAPTER TEN

An hour later, we had finished the blueberry pancakes I had made. Pete liked his food. Luckily, I'm a damn good cook. You can't be Italian and not learn a thing or two about food.

I was clearing the table when Pete said, "So. You still need to get a few rings back?"

No wonder I loved this man. No lectures, no recriminations. No mention of the police. Especially that.

"One or two," I said. It felt good, telling the truth. Rather an unfamiliar feeling, but good.

"You should have told me in the first place," Pete said. "Might have saved you and the masked man some trouble."

I raised an eyebrow hopefully.

"I can think of other ways to get those rings back. Easier ways," he said.

"Give," I said.

Pete shrugged. His big footballer body rocked the wooden chair he was sitting in.

"I work for a newspaper, remember? Just tell these women the *Steeltown Star* is doing an article on precious jewelry in the city, and we want to feature theirs. Have them bring the rings in to the store to be examined and photographed. Then you can do the substitutions and give them back. We all live happily ever after."

I felt my jaw drop and my mouth open. "Pete, that's brilliant! Can you pull it off with a *Star* photographer?"

"Sure. Ben owes me. You can give the ladies a professional photo of their trophy jewelry and tell them you don't know when the story is going to run. But I might be able to get the Life section to do an actual story. I'll try."

I bounced around the island and slid myself into Pete's lap.

"Did I ever tell you that I am just crazy about you?" I ruffled his wavy dark-blond hair.

Pete grinned, and my heart turned over.

"Back atcha," he said. "Against my better judgment, I might add."

I swiveled my head to look behind me. "Looky there. I cleared the table."

Pete laughed. His eyes dazzled. "Think it will hold us?"

I like dessert after breakfast.

* * *

We had a nice morning. I said so to Pete while climbing out of bed for the second time.

He came up behind me.

"Personally, I object to the word *nice*," he said, fondling parts of me with his hands. "I am not feeling the least bit nice at the moment. Although these are… rather…nice…"

"Stop that," I said, smacking his hands down. "I'm trying to get dressed."

The phone rang. It was my oldest and best friend, Lainy McSwain.

"Hiya, Sugar," she said happily. "Whatcha doin'?"

"Lainy!" I screamed into the phone. "It's so good to hear your voice!"

"You too, Cupcake. I'm gonna be in town for two weeks solid, so get used to it. But first, what's this I hear about a new stallion in your paddock?"

I looked over at Pete, who was pulling on his pants, and smiled.

Lainy—Elaine, to her parents—was my best friend when I was growing up.

In high school, we drove the nuns crazy by passing notes back and forth and generally testing most of the Ten Commandments.

Then something earthshaking happened. After high school, Elaine went to university in Guelph, where she discovered country music and big hair. The University of Guelph is the home of the world-class Ontario Agricultural College and is often fondly referred to as Cow College or Moo U.

Elaine—now Lainy—took to the country music scene like a horse to hay, and the rest is history.

Her first gig was with The Cow College Critters. They did the local bar scene for a few years. Then they changed a few of the players and got a new name, Lainy McSwain and the Lonesome Doves.

Two years ago, Lainy made it big on the country charts with her solo hit, "You Done Me Wrong, So I Done You In."

This year she opened for Shania Twain and captured two more golds with "That Ain't No Cow, It's Ma Maw" and "Don't Give Me No Hickey, You Hick From North Bay."

Not only is Lainy's voice big. At five foot ten, so is the rest of her. Lainy has country-singer hair and country-singer boobs—all real. She is one heck of a red-haired, broad-shouldered, big-hipped, man-lovin' superstar.

I love her to bits.

"When do you get in?" I said.

"Next Thursday, late. I'll be at your place Friday. I promised Pinky I'd play at her Halloween party. It's supposed to be a surprise for Ben. Can I bunk at your place for the weekend?"

"Sure thing, Lainy." I looked over at Pete, who was bent over, doing up his shoes, and wondered if he'd mind a little company in the condo.

"Don't bother kickin' your stallion out, darlin'. I want to get to know him good."

I smiled. Lainy always could read my mind.

CHAPTER ELEVEN

*B*urglary *for Dummies* will also feature a chapter called "Accomplice Relations." Specifically, circumstances under which it is perfectly reasonable to kill your accomplice.

It was Saturday morning at my place, and Pete had the newspaper in his hand. He waved to me as I came into the kitchen.

"You may want to see this. Or not. I think Nico has gone rogue."

I grabbed the paper. The headline read:

Lone Rearranger Gives 5 Stars to
Red Hill Residence

Country Club Drive residents Phil and Myla Tanner were delighted to return home Friday night and find they had been targeted by the Lone Rearranger.

"I'm just so thrilled," said Mrs. Tanner. "He didn't rearrange a thing! Just left a white mask on the Italian sectional and a red rose on the coffee table. He loved the room! Wait till my friends hear."

"This guy has class," said Mr. Tanner.

This is believed to be the first living room left completely untouched by the Lone Rearranger. Police are baffled by why anyone would—

"NICO!" I screamed.

I was just about to grab the phone when it started ringing.

"It's Sammy," the caller said. "We need to talk."

Oops.

* * *

We arranged to meet at the chicken coop.

I brought reinforcements. Tiff and Nico. Okay, so I was a teeny bit chicken to meet Sammy alone. At the chicken coop. Bad pun, I know.

I drove and picked up the others. We beat Sammy to the site. I used my key to unlock the door.

"Wow," said Tiff. "I've never been here before."

"Cool cigs," said Nico. "Want a pack, Tiff?" He reached for a carton on the nearest pile.

"No!" I hissed. "No taking anything! It's not ours to take."

Nico looked at me strangely. Then he grinned.

"Okay, I know that sounds dumb," I admitted. Ownership of said items was rather debatable at the moment.

Then Sammy came through the door. For a moment, he was a scary silhouette, backlit by the sunlight behind him. Then he stepped forward, and his features came into view.

His gaze swept over Tiff and me and landed on Nico.

"You," he said, pointing a bony finger. "You're the mask guy."

Nico squirmed. "I was only having some fun, Uncle Sammy. I miss the old days."

"Fun? Are you nuts? Pulling fake robberies? Don't you know how that can mess up the real ones?"

Time for me to step in. "They weren't fake, Sammy. This is my fault. I was stealing back the fake stones that Carmine used. Nico was my wingman. Until he went rogue." I turned and gave him the evil eye.

Sammy slapped a palm to his forehead. "Wait. I can't keep up with this shit. Take me through it from the start."

Tiff explained the good parts. She was actually very cool in an emergency. Good to know for the future.

I stepped in when it was necessary. Like when it looked like Sammy was going to strangle Nico.

"Holy shit, Nico. You got the brains of a long-dead lake trout. Don't you EVER leave those white masks behind on a job again. They can pick up the smallest bits of DNA on those things. Miriam will bat your ears if she finds out."

Nico looked suitable chastened. Aunt Miriam had a way with ears.

But all in all, it wasn't a bad meeting. In fact, the last part was pretty good.

"Here, I got something for you," Sammy said. He dug into a pocket and came out with a memory stick. "Play that on your laptop. You'll find it quite entertaining—and useful. Miriam gave me a little help. I think you'll like that part."

I reached for it as he continued to stare at me.

"Carmine?" I said hopefully.

Sammy smiled. It wasn't a nice smile. "With a curvy little blond gal that isn't his wife."

Holy shit, indeed.

CHAPTER TWELVE

I viewed the video in the privacy of my home office. Yup. What we had here was first-class blackmail material. YouTube gold.

I convinced Pete to make the trip with carrots and a side order of guilt. The guilt was easy.

"I just spent a week with your parents in Florida. Surely you can spare a day to meet my rotten cousin in New York."

Pete sighed. "If by *meet* you mean *take down*, count me in."

Man, I loved this guy.

We got through security at the airport without any trouble. Pete had his NEXUS card and I had my—well, one of my passports.

"So what's the plan?" Pete said as he buckled up.

"I sort of need you to pretend to be a bad guy," I said. "Think you can do that?"

Pete snorted, and it kind of scared me. "Sweetheart, you have no idea."

Then the plane took off.

Once we reached LaGuardia, Pete took command. He flagged a New York taxi like it was second nature to him. Of course, because it was Pete, one came immediately. If it had been me, we would have been waiting until tax time.

"First we hit Schwarz. Then—what's the address?"

I gave him the address. "What's *Schwarz*?"

He grinned. "You'll see." He gave instructions to the driver.

After we'd finished our business at Schwarz, Pete flagged another cab.

"You're pretty cool about this," I said. "Any reason I should know about?"

Pete put his arm around my shoulders. "I know this city. And I wasn't always a pussycat reporter, you know. You got to be tough in the pros. I just don't get to show it off much anymore."

I looked at the big guy beside me and brought my hand up to test his bicep. "You've been working out with Luca, haven't you?"

He grinned. "If you call ten rounds in a ring with a stubborn-ass mob enforcer working out, then yeah."

"Luca isn't an *enforcer*," I said.

"Well, he outta be. He sure can hit."

And so can you, I thought to myself, if you can stay in the ring with Luca. All of a sudden, I felt very safe.

The cab stopped outside the door of Venetian Jewelers. I hauled my butt out of the car. Pete handed me the laptop. "Best I keep my hands free," he said.

Damn but he had good instincts.

Either there was no alarm on the street door or it wasn't working. We walked right in. Venetian Jewelers was old school. Lots of oak cabinetry with boring beige walls to match. Nico would be in despair.

I walked up to the gum-chewing schoolgirl at the counter. She looked bored. I felt mildly sorry for her, so I decided to make her unbored.

"I'm Carmine's cousin. You've got thirty seconds to take me to him before I start blowing the place. Get my drift?" I find it best to talk in language that can be easily understood by the natives.

Pete looked a little surprised though. Guess I should have warned him.

Miss Bored Universe glanced at me briefly and then cocked her head toward the back of the store. Her gelled hair hardly moved. She never missed a chew.

I walked around the counter and to the door to the back. Miss B buzzed it open, and I turned the knob.

Carmine was sitting behind a wooden desk, eating a slice of pizza. And yup, he looked just like I remembered him. Scrawny little bastard with black hair, a pointy face and bony hands. Did I mention I used to call him Ratface?

When he looked up and saw me, he sneered. He also wasn't alone.

"Oh Christ—YOU guys?" I couldn't believe it.

Joey, Bertoni and the guy named Lou were also munching away. I could smell pepperoni and lots of hot cheese. Bertoni put down his pizza and wiped his greasy hands on his shirt. Ick.

Joey groaned when he saw me. Then his eyes swept past me to Pete. Joey stiffened.

"Hey Carm! He's got a heater in his pocket!"

Bertoni yelled, and there was a whirl of action as everyone reached somewhere on their body for something.

In a flash, the room was still. Carm, Bertoni, Joey, Lou and Pete all had guns pointing at each other.

"Oh for goodness' sake," I said. Pete stood there holding the gun he had just bought. Yup, from the toy store.

"What kind of heater is that? I never seen it before." Bertoni stepped forward. He was curious.

"It's a Canadian Military Special," Pete said. He held it naturally, like he'd been doing it every day of his life. "New. Made for the high Arctic. Never fails."

I nearly guffawed but held it back.

"You bringing guns down from Canada into the States now? Isn't that kind of backward?" Lou said this.

Silence.

"Oh, I get what you mean," I said finally. I turned to Pete to explain. "Usually we move guns from Buffalo to Toronto. Luca handles that side of the—wait a minute. You didn't hear me just say that."

"We got you outnumbered, man," Carmine said. "Four against one." He practically swaggered.

"What the hell are you doing?" Now I was mad. "We're cousins! We can't kill each other. You got any idea what Vince would do if one of us got shot? And Big Sally? Not to mention Aunt Miriam."

Joey flinched at the mention of Aunt Miriam.

"What's the deal with Aunt Miriam?" Pete asked.

"Smelly yellow soap," Joey murmured. He shivered.

"Take it from me. You don't want to mess with her." Bertoni looked pale. His greasy hair was standing on end.

"So put the guns down, all of you." I tried to make my voice sound like Miriam's. "There's no need for violence. We just have to come to an arrangement."

Carmine snorted. "So you want the gems back. Tough. Make me."

I turned to him. This was my big scene, and dammit, I was going to enjoy it.

"Oh, darlin', I will. Or rather, Aunt Miriam will. Pete, help me with the laptop."

Pete hesitated. He looked around the group.

"Put the guns down, I said!" I shrieked this time and swung my arms about. Gad, I was getting more like Miriam with every minute.

The guns went down. All of them.

"Jeez. You guys are so anachronistic."

"What the fuck does that mean?" Bertoni frowned.

I rolled my eyes. "It means so last century. Or the ones before." I opened the laptop on Carmine's desk and pressed a few keys.

"Now Carmine, move up front here and pay close attention to this video. You might know the people."

Everyone came closer. You could almost hear each individual breath. Until I turned up the volume, and then you could only hear the heavy breathing and moans coming from the laptop.

"Oh Carmy! Do it—do it—ahhhhh…"

"I'm doin' it, babe—I'm doin' it!"

"Faster, Carmy! Faster—don't stop…"

All eyes were glued to the screen.

"Oh, gross," said Lou.

"Holy shit!" yelled Carmine. "How did you get that?"

"Carm, that ain't your wife. Tracy's not a blond." Bertoni was confused.

"How the heck is she doing that?" Pete was staring at the video with far too much interest. Okay, time to pull the plug.

The picture faded, and Aunt Miriam's serene face came onscreen.

"Now Carmine," she said. "You've been a bad boy. It isn't nice to steal from your Auntie Miriam. Or from the family. So here's what we're going to do. Big Sally loves his daughter Tracy very much, and I don't think he would be too happy to see this video of her husband with a hooker up on YouTube, do you? No, I didn't think so. Give Gina back the gems, Carmine. All of them. There's a good boy.

"Oh, and don't even think of destroying this laptop because I have many more copies of this video back in Hamilton.

"Say hi to your mother for me."

Then she was gone.

"Fuckity fuck," said Carmine. His eyes bugged from his face.

"I see what you mean about Aunt Miriam," Pete said. "That face. That voice. It isn't normal."

He shivered.

Carmine grabbed me by the arm. "You gotta give me that flash drive. Christ! If Tracy sees this…"

I tried to shake him off. "Big Sally should scare you more. Are you nuts, cheating on his daughter? What the crap were you thinking?"

"You gotta help me get those vids back or I'm a dead man!" He tried to grab my other arm, but I backed away.

"Hey! Let go of her," Pete growled and moved forward.

"Let go of me, Carm. For crissake, I haven't got time for this!" I whacked his head with my free hand. "Just give me back the stones."

"I don't have them," Carmine mumbled. "I have to get them back from some guy."

I rolled my eyes. There was always "some guy."

"You have a week, Carm. One week to get those rocks back to me. But now I have to get home in time to meet up with Lainy. She's here with the Doves, and I don't get to see her very often anymore. Do a turf war with Aunt Miriam on your own time. I got a plane to catch."

Silence. *Why silence? What did I say?* Everybody stopped moving.

"Lainy? Lainy McSwain, the country singer?" Joey asked.

I nodded.

"You know her?"

This was weird. "She's my best friend," I said.

"Why didn't we know that, Carm? Why the fuck didn't we know that?" Joey said. He waved his arms through the air.

"Are you kidding me? I LOVE Lainy McSwain! Can you get us tickets or something?" the goon named Lou piped up.

I looked over at Pete, who had turned toward the wall. By the way his back was shaking, I figured he was silently sniggering.

"I can do better than that," I said slowly. Then my voice picked up. "She's playing at Aunt Pinky's Halloween party on Friday night. You can come as my guests and meet her in person."

"Holy shit. Listen, there's this chick I know in North Tonawanda—"

"Yes, Joey, you can bring the chick from North Tonawanda. Jeesh."

"Is she going to play 'You Done Me Wrong, So I Done You In'? I love that song," said Bertoni.

Figures.

I scanned my watch. "She'll play the song. Look. I hate to break this up, but we gotta make like a banana and peel. Meet me at my place at six on Friday. I'll email the address. We'll go to the party together. Oh, and don't forget to bring the rocks you owe me."

"Will Aunt Miriam be there?" Joey shivered.

I closed the laptop and picked it up. "And wear a costume! It's a costume party."

I managed to get Pete and his toy gun out the door before he expired on the floor.

CHAPTER THIRTEEN

We caught the plane. We even got home to my place in one piece. Well, two pieces, as there were two of us.

I was feeling good about the rocks. Carmine would bring them back to Hamilton himself. That meant he got to take the risk of carrying them across the border for a change.

Then Lainy called to say her flight had been delayed and she'd meet me at Pinky's. We'd get together after the show and have a whole two weeks to gab. I filled her in on what had been happening lately. She was looking forward to meeting the "stallion in my paddock."

Things were looking up.

* * *

Pete arrived at my door on Friday night dressed as a Roman centurion. He had on a tunic with a breastplate that looked to be covered with aluminum foil. And he was armed. There was a dagger at his waist and one down the side of his boot. Another weapon hung from his belt.

I leaned against the doorjamb and did my best Mae West impression.

"Is that a broadsword on your belt or are you just glad to see me?"

Pete hooted.

Then he reached for me. "I'm always glad to see you, babe. And that is one heck of a slave-girl costume. Like the image. And the one-shoulder getup."

"I'm not a slave girl!" Jeesh. Like I would ever want to be that. "Slave girls don't wear jeweled brooches. I'm a Roman senator's daughter." Close enough to a mob king's goddaughter, I figured. I wondered if Cicero would agree.

Pete was still staring at the costume.

"Say, if I remove the brooch, does this toga thing come apart?"

"That'll have to wait." I lowered my voice. "Joey and the gang are here. But the girlfriend couldn't make it. She didn't have a passport."

"Carm brought the rocks?"

I nodded. "All's well, if not exactly sane." I started to pull Pete by the hand into the living room. Then I stopped and turned back.

"Oh, and don't laugh," I warned.

Good thing I warned him. We entered the room. I felt Pete tense beside me and then shake a bit.

"Are we going to a rodeo?" he whispered. I slapped his arm.

The boys from Buffalo had gotten into the theme of things. In fact, it kind of looked like they might be getting ready to herd buffalo. Carmine, Joey, Lou and Bertoni were dressed as cowboys.

I don't know if you have ever seen a bunch of New York hoods pretending to be Wild West outlaws. Or marshals—Lou did have a star pinned to his chest.

Let me tell you, it does take some imagination. But if you have ever seen old western shows on television, you may remember that big guy called Hoss.

Joey made a perfect Hoss. I almost expected the *Bonanza* theme song to come piping through the walls.

"Howdy," said Pete, grinning from ear to ear. "Lookin' good."

The others tipped their ten-gallon hats and nodded. They were dressed in blue jeans, plaid shirts and leather chaps. They had matching red bandannas. And boots with spurs. Looked a little strange with the tattoos.

I could tell Pete was trying to hold back a snigger. I followed his gaze. Bertoni had pasted a droopy black mustache on his face.

"This being the first time we meet Lainy and the Lonesome Doves," said Joey, "we figured we should dress the part."

"On account of their being country an' western." Lou nodded.

The fake Texas accents were a bit jarring, but I gave them A+ for effort.

"Stupid Canada. Couldn't bring our heaters over the border, so we have to wear these fake things." Bertoni pointed to the toy revolver in his holster. He sounded disgusted.

I wondered if they were purchased at the same store Pete's so-called Canadian Military Special came from.

"You a warrior of some sort? What do you call those dudes?" Carmine said.

Pete was a whirl of arms. Daggers appeared in each hand. "I'm a Roman centurion. Nobody move, or I'll fill you full of bronze."

I rolled my eyes. "Time to go, children. Joey, you guys follow my car."

CHAPTER FOURTEEN

Pinky Palmerston had made what we in the family called a good marriage. In high school, she was a knockout cheerleader who hooked up with a really smart guy. They got engaged at eighteen. When Ben was accepted into McMaster's medical school, my uncle Vince footed the bill. So we have a surgeon in the family as well as a lawyer. Which is really very handy. Don't ask why.

Ben and Pinky live on a country estate just outside Hamilton. It was château chic before fake French châteaus became the rage.

It is also about as big as Versailles. When you push back the furniture, the great room alone can easily handle a crowd of a hundred.

When we got there, the place was already rocking. Tony, one of her sons, manned the double front doors, keeping out the riffraff. He looked like Pinky— tall and slim, with Italian-movie-star good looks. The slick suit he was wearing had to have cost at least two thousand bucks.

Tony's face split into a grin when he saw me.

"Hey, Gina. You behind the whole Lone Rearranger thing?"

I started. "Don't spread that around, Tony! Jeesh, I'm in enough shit."

"Another Tony?" Pete said innocently.

My cousin and I exchanged knowing smiles. My other cousin Tony had been taken out by a New York connection. He wasn't much of a loss.

"You're not really Italian unless you have at least two cousins named Tony," I explained patiently.

"And one uncle," added Tony.

Pete put out his hand.

Tony shook it. "Cool costume. Like the sword."

I pulled Pete into the marble foyer before he could start demonstrating his weapons. Carmine and the Buffalo boys shuffled in behind us.

Country music was coming from the two-story space just beyond the plaster columns in front of us. Live palm trees at least fifteen feet tall flanked the columns.

We entered the immense party room beyond. It was dimly lit, so it took a second for my eyes to adjust. When they did, I nearly fell over.

"Oh no. Look!"

"Oh Christ." Pete started to chortle. Then he howled.

In front of us was a guy carrying a bottle of wine. He was dressed in black and wearing a white Zorro mask. Behind him was another guy wearing a similar white mask.

"I count three. No, four."

"Five. Here comes Nico."

Even with the mask, you couldn't miss his bleached hair.

Nico grabbed me in a bear hug. "Gina, can you believe it? I'm a superstar! It's the costume of the year! Of course, I had to wear it. Who knows when I'll get the chance again? And look at all the others. I tell you, it's brilliant. Such a commendation. I'm chuffed."

My eyes could hardly focus. Every second man at the party was dressed up as the Lone Rearranger. Some were dark-haired and some were bald. There were thin ones and pot-bellied ones. There had to be at least ten. No, make that twelve.

Thirteen. There was even a reverse Lone Rearranger. He was all in white with a black mask.

"Is that—oh my god, it's Stoner and Toke. Hi, Stoner! Isn't that cute!" Nico pointed.

The black standard poodle was wearing a white mask.

One especially tall guy was wearing a white mask and a black cape.

"Oh god, I need that cape. Why didn't I think of a cape? I wonder if he'll sell it." Nico took off in the direction of the cape man. I didn't hold out much hope for the poor guy's chances.

Pete was bent over, wheezing.

"You have to stop laughing like that. You'll hurt yourself on your sword." I fussed about him.

"It's your family," he said, straightening. Tears were running down his face. "They slay me."

"They better not!" I said firmly.

The band was whipping up to a crescendo. Lainy's voice was coming through loud, clear and gorgeous.

"You done me wrong, so I done you in
The cops are comin' to take me in
Two pumps in the chest—yeah, I know
  it's a sin
But you done me wrong, an' I'd do it ag'in
Oh yeah, babe
Bye-bye, babe."

Pete put an arm around my shoulders. "Catchy lyrics," he said.

"Kind of a family motto," I replied.

He pulled me closer. "Another one?"

I cocked my head sideways. "Aunt Miriam always says, *Divorce, never. Murder, maybe.*"

Pete smirked. "Fine by me. I play for keeps."

The music stopped. Then the cheers and whistles started up.

Lainy left the stage and headed our way. As always, every male eye in the place was glued to her brown suede skirt as she sashayed over. Not to mention the big red hair and the checkered cowgirl shirt that was straining at the buttons. Good thing she was so darn nice or it would be hard not to be jealous.

"Hey, girlfriend! It's so damned good to see ya."

She gave me a big happy hug. Then she eyed the big guy beside me and whispered, "I'll get to know your sugar later. But first..."

She turned to the cousins.

"So...which one of these hombres is your cousin Carmine, Gina?"

I pointed.

Lainy went up to Carmine, who was bug-eyed with hero worship. She grabbed his bolo tie with her right hand and yanked it, pulling him over until they were nose to nose. Or rather, more like nose to boob. Lainy is over six feet tall in her boots and built like Dolly Parton, so she kind of towered over Carmine.

"Now listen to me, cowboy. You mess with my gal pal again, and I got a six-shooter with your name on it. You get me?"

Carmine nodded vigorously. I think he was having trouble breathing.

Lainy let go of the bolo and pushed him back. "Just so we understand each other. I'm a no-nonsense kind of girl, if you get my drift. But just to prove I can be friendly, like, what's your favorite song that I do?"

Carmine was still wide-eyed and gasping. He didn't seem to be able to talk.

"He likes 'You're Roadkill on My Highway of Life,'" said Joey.

"It's up next," Lainy said. She winked at me and turned to go back to the band.

"Wow." Bertoni was drooling. "Is she ever *hot*."

"Oh, look," Pete said wickedly. "Here comes Aunt Miriam."

They vanished.

ACKNOWLEDGMENTS

Many thanks to my first readers, Cathy Astolfo and Cheryl Freedman, who laugh easily and generously show me when I hit a funny bone.

Thanks also to my Italian relatives still living (you know who you are), a lively and fun-loving bunch. Thanks as well to some of those now dead (and note that I waited to publish this until now).

Finally, I am particularly grateful to the superb team at Orca Books, including my editor, Bob Tyrrell, along with Dayle Sutherland, Leslie Bootle and the rest of the marketing department. They make every step in the publishing process a pleasure.

Although **MELODIE CAMPBELL** got her start writing comedy, her work has appeared in *Alfred Hitchcock Mystery Magazine*, *Canadian Living*, *The Toronto Star*, *The Globe and Mail* and many other publications. *The Goddaughter's Revenge* is Melodie's fifth published novel and second in the Rapid Reads series (*The Goddaughter*, Orca/Raven Books, 2012). She lives in Oakville, Ontario, and can be found at www.melodiecampbell.com.

978-1-4598-0125-7 $9.95 pb

I sat down on the edge of a concrete planter and tried to remain calm… But three bullets and a river of blood can mess up a girl's composure.

Gina Gallo would like nothing better than to run her little jewelry shop. Unfortunately, she's also "the Goddaughter," and, as she tells her friend Pete, "You don't get to choose your relatives."

When her cousin Tony is shot by rival mobsters, Gina is reluctantly recruited to carry the hot gems he was carrying back to Buffalo. Then the worst happens: the gems get stolen. Pete and Gina have no choice but to steal them back.